This Igloo book belongs to:

....

igloo

Published in 2011
by Igloo Books Ltd
Cottage Farm
Sywell
NN6 0BJ
www.igloo-books.com

10 9 8 7 6 5 4 3 2
ISBN 978-0-85734-459-5

Illustrated by Ted Dawson, Gary Rees and Geoff Walton
Printed and manufactured in China

Stories for Boys

igloo

Contents

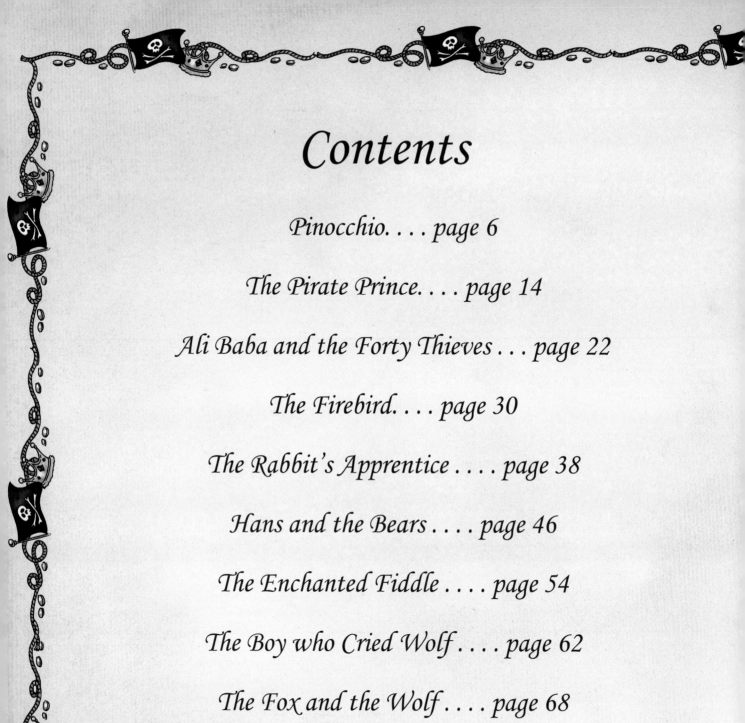

Pinocchio

Once upon a time, an old carpenter, called Geppetto, lived all by himself. He was so lonely, he decided to make a wooden puppet to keep him company.

In his workshop, Geppetto carved a little wooden head, a wooden body and wooden arms and legs. Then he dressed the puppet in clothes, like a real boy. "I will call him Pinocchio," said Geppetto. The old carpenter looked at the puppet. "I wish you were real," he said. "I have always wanted a son."

Suddenly, by some strange, unseen magic, the wooden puppet began to move. Geppetto stared in amazement as it jumped up from the work bench and began to run around the workshop, shouting and waving its arms.

Geppetto was overjoyed. He did not understand why his wooden puppet had come to life, but he was very happy. "Pinocchio," said Geppetto, "I am your father and tomorrow you will go to school. Maybe, one day, if you learn enough, you will become a real boy."

That night, when Pinocchio went to bed, he dreamed that a beautiful fairy visited him. "I am the Blue Fairy who looks after all boys – real, or wooden," she said. "I have brought you a friend to help you to be good." The Blue Fairy waved her wand and a tiny cricket appeared.

The cricket was able to speak. "Hello, Pinocchio," it said. "I will be your friend and help you to behave properly, like a real boy. Tomorrow, we shall go to school together."

The next morning, Pinocchio went downstairs with the cricket. Geppetto was very proud that his little wooden son was going to school. "Here are five gold coins to buy school books with," he said. "It's all the money I have in the world, so spend it wisely."

"Yes, Father," said Pinocchio. But the wooden puppet was lying. He did not want to go to school, or spend the money on school books. Suddenly, Pinocchio's wooden nose grew longer. Geppetto looked at it and frowned. "Pinocchio," he said, "why is your nose growing?" But the puppet just grabbed the gold coins, shoved them into his pocket and ran out of the door.

The clever cricket knew that the puppet's nose had changed because he had told a lie. From that moment on, each time Pinocchio lied, his nose grew longer.

Meanwhile, outside the house, Pinocchio heard lovely music. "Let's go to school," said the cricket, but Pinocchio ignored him and followed the music, which led to a travelling puppet theater.

"I am going to stay here and become a performer," said Pinocchio. "My father won't mind." But when he said this, Pinocchio's nose grew, which meant he was lying.

The cricket tried to stop Pinocchio, but the puppet would not listen.
Instead of going to school, he travelled with the theater to a distant land,
near the sea.

Poor Geppetto looked everywhere for his precious, wooden son.
But Pinocchio was nowhere to be found.

After many days, the cricket persuaded Pinocchio to go back home.
They set off and Pinocchio jangled Geppetto's five, gold coins in his pockets,
as he walked.

Nearby, a cunning cat and a sly fox heard the money jangling.
"Where are you going, little wooden boy?" they asked. Pinocchio told them
that he was going home to see his father. "Your father will make you go to
school, when you could be having fun in the Land of Play," said the sly fox.

"However," said the cat. Nobody who has any money can get in. Money
isn't allowed in the Land of Play."

Pinocchio gave the fox and the cat all of his money. He would not listen to the cricket who told him not to. "Tell me the way to the Land of Play," begged Pinocchio, "I want to go there now."

The cat and the fox told Pinocchio where to go. Then they ran off, laughing at how they had tricked the silly puppet out of his money.

"Please, Pinocchio, go home to your father," pleaded the cricket. "I don't want to see my father," snapped the puppet. Suddenly, his nose grew longer. Pinocchio secretly missed Geppetto, but he refused to go home.

The Land of Play was a huge fair. There were sweets and rides and lots of games to play. It was filled with children who didn't want to go to school and Pinocchio spent many weeks there.

Meanwhile, Geppetto was sick with worry. He searched all over the land for Pinocchio, but there was no sign of him anywhere. Finally, Geppetto reached the sea. "Pinocchio must have crossed the water," he thought. Geppetto built a raft to look for his son. However, far out on the ocean, the raft was swallowed by a huge shark and Geppetto found himself in its belly.

In the Land of Play, Pinocchio didn't notice the days passing until his ears began to feel strange. They were long and floppy, like donkey's ears. Then, when he looked behind him, Pinocchio noticed that he had grown a donkey's tail.

"All children who stay here turn into donkeys," said the cricket. "We must escape, before you become one, too, Pinocchio."

However, the gates of the Land of Play were shut. The only way out was by sea, so Pinocchio and the cricket jumped into the water.

Great waves rolled and the wild sea tossed the pair up and down. After many hours, a huge shark swam by and swallowed the exhausted friends.

It was dark inside the shark's belly. Suddenly, Pinocchio heard a voice – it was Geppetto! "I'm sorry that I lied and ran away, Father," sobbed Pinocchio.

Geppetto hugged his wooden son. "I forgive you," he said. They all danced for joy and the movement gave the shark such a belly-ache, it spat them out and they were washed up on the shore.

After that, Pinocchio promised to be good and this time, his nose didn't grow. Instead, the Blue Fairy appeared. "Pinocchio, you have learned to tell the truth," she said. "Now you are a real boy."

Pinocchio felt the donkey ears and tail disappear. Suddenly, his wooden body was soft and warm. He was a real boy! Pinocchio, Geppetto and the cricket returned home and lived in peace and happiness ever after.

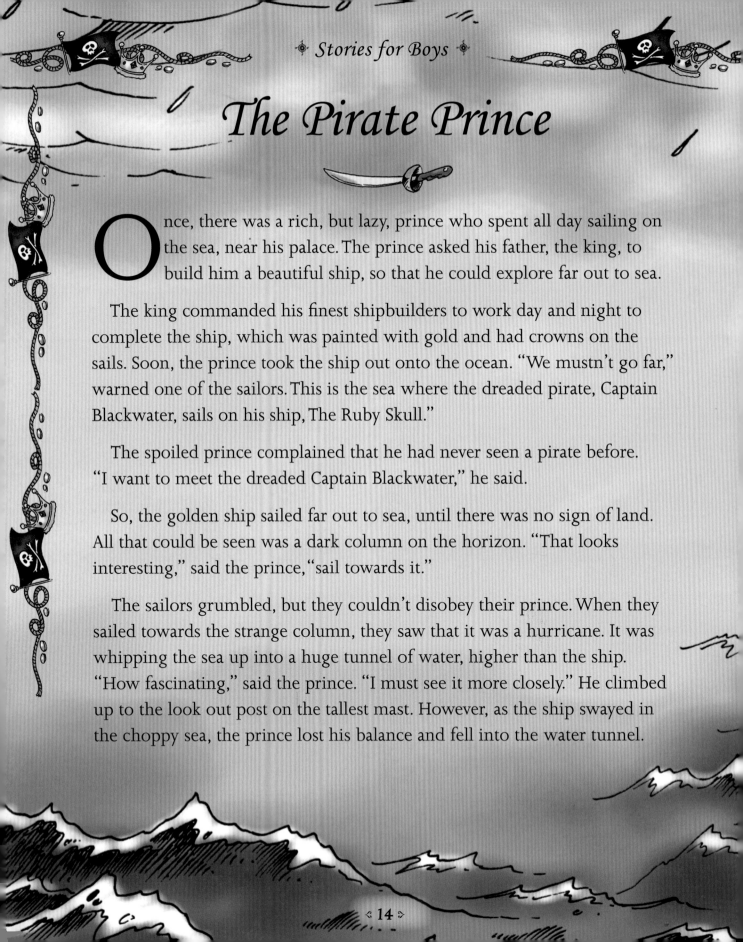

The Pirate Prince

Once, there was a rich, but lazy, prince who spent all day sailing on the sea, near his palace. The prince asked his father, the king, to build him a beautiful ship, so that he could explore far out to sea.

The king commanded his finest shipbuilders to work day and night to complete the ship, which was painted with gold and had crowns on the sails. Soon, the prince took the ship out onto the ocean. "We mustn't go far," warned one of the sailors. This is the sea where the dreaded pirate, Captain Blackwater, sails on his ship, The Ruby Skull."

The spoiled prince complained that he had never seen a pirate before. "I want to meet the dreaded Captain Blackwater," he said.

So, the golden ship sailed far out to sea, until there was no sign of land. All that could be seen was a dark column on the horizon. "That looks interesting," said the prince, "sail towards it."

The sailors grumbled, but they couldn't disobey their prince. When they sailed towards the strange column, they saw that it was a hurricane. It was whipping the sea up into a huge tunnel of water, higher than the ship. "How fascinating," said the prince. "I must see it more closely." He climbed up to the look out post on the tallest mast. However, as the ship swayed in the choppy sea, the prince lost his balance and fell into the water tunnel.

The prince was sucked into the hurricane and carried far away until, at last, the fierce wind died down and the prince was dropped into the sea. He swam with all his might and eventually reached a deserted island.

The prince lived on the empty island for many months, growing lean and fit. One day, a big, fast-looking ship sailed past. The prince waved and shouted at the top of his voice. The ship stopped and he swam out to it.

A rope dropped down the side of the great ship and the prince climbed up. Someone helped him, but instead of grabbing onto a hand, the prince found he was holding a hook. It belonged to none other than Captain Blackwater, the most fearsome pirate on the seven seas. The ship was his famous vessel, The Ruby Skull.

"We have come to this island to maroon a group of mutineers," said the captain. "One of them was my second in command. If you can defeat him in a swordfight, you can take his place."

The mutinous sailor was a wicked-looking man. Someone threw the prince a sword and he fought the sailor on the deck of The Ruby Skull. With a clever flick of his sword, the prince sent the man tumbling over the side of the ship and the pirates gave a big cheer.

"There is a wicked sultan in these parts who kidnaps men from the coast and sells them as slaves," said Captain Blackwater. "We plunder his ships and set the slaves free. Will you join us, stranger?"

The prince had no choice but to join Captain Blackwater's crew and became a pirate. They sailed the seas and attacked all the sultan's ships they could find. They stole all the gold and jewels from the sultan and they set all the sultan's slaves free. The prince became a hardworking sailor and a brave fighter. He soon lost his spoiled ways.

One day, news reached Captain Blackwater that the sultan had sent boats out to capture a king, who was sailing nearby.

"This king sails the ocean in a golden ship, with crowns on the sails," said the captain. "It's said that he searches for his long-lost son."

When the prince heard this, he knew this king must be his father. "I know this king," said the prince. "If we can reach him before the sultan does, we will all be rich."

"The sultan's ship is twice as big as The Ruby Skull," said Captain Blackwater. "We must reach the king's ship first."

The captain set sail for the golden ship but, as it came within sight, the prince saw that the sultan's towering vessel had already reached it. The sultan's men had jumped aboard the king's ship and taken him hostage.

Captain Blackwater waited until the dead of night, then he sailed up close and sneaked aboard with all his crew.

When the sultan's men woke up, they found they were being invaded. They drew their weapons and fought the pirates. In the chaos of the battle, the prince searched the lower deck of the ship until he found a locked room. Forcing it open, he found the king inside. The king drew his sword. "You won't take me alive, pirate," he roared.

"I'm here to rescue you, father," said the prince. The king recognized his son and they hugged, joyfully. Together, the king and the prince rushed to fight with Captain Blackwater and his men. They helped the pirates to defeat the sultan's crew and capture the huge ship.

When the battle was over, Captain Blackwater was very surprised to find that a member of his crew was a prince. However, he was a little worried that the king might punish him for his pirate ways.

The next day, the king, the prince and the pirate all sailed back to the palace together. The king was so delighted to have his son back, he made Captain Blackwater head of his fleet. The captain was so proud, he decided to give up being a pirate altogether.

After that, the sultan never troubled the king, or the pirate prince again and everyone lived happily ever after.

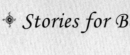

Ali Baba and the Forty Thieves

Many years ago, there were two brothers called Ali Baba and Kassim, who lived in a great, eastern city. Ali Baba was hard-working and honest, but his brother, Kassim, was cruel and greedy. Kassim took all the money that the brothers earned and Ali Baba hardly ever had enough to buy food.

One day, when Ali Baba was out gathering wood in the forest, he heard the sound of many voices. Peering through the trees, he saw a crowd of forty evil-looking thieves carrying large sacks. The leader of the thieves called out, "Quick, we must take this stolen gold into our magic cave."

The thieves were standing by a rocky wall and Ali Baba couldn't see any opening in it. "Open, Sesame," cried the leader. Suddenly, the rocks parted to show an entrance into a cave, filled with treasure. The thieves put the gold in the cave and then the leader cried "Close, Sesame." The hole in the rock disappeared and the thieves ran away, laughing.

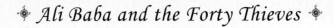

When the thieves had gone, Ali Baba stood in front of the rock. "Open, Sesame!" he shouted. Sure enough, the rock opened to reveal the magic cave.

Inside, the cave was full of gold, jewels and all kinds of treasure. Ali Baba put some of the coins in his pocket. When he turned to go, he found he was trapped inside. The rock had closed behind him. "Open, Sesame," he yelled and the rock opened again.

Ali Baba rushed out of the cave. "Close, Sesame!" he cried and the huge rock sealed the entrance.

When Ali Baba got home, his brother, Kassim, asked him where he had got the coins. Reluctantly, Ali Baba told him about the thieves, the cave and the magic word.

Greedy Kassim wanted all the treasure for himself. That night, he travelled to the cave and called out, "Open, Sesame." The cave opened and Kassim rushed in and stuffed his pockets with treasure. Then he realised that he was shut in. "I'll just say the magic word," thought Kassim. But he had forgotten it. "Open, semolina," he said. "Open, sugary." But, try as he might, Kassim couldn't make the rock move. He was trapped in the cave all night.

The next morning, the forty thieves opened the cave and found Kassim. "Stealing our treasure, are you?" said the leader. "Tie him up and leave him here," he said to this men.

The next day, Ali Baba was worried that Kassim had not returned. He went to the cave and used the magic word to open it. Kassim was lying inside, tied up and helpless. Ali Baba untied his brother and they fled, just as the thieves were returning to the cave. The thieves chased them all the way to the city. Ali Baba and Kassim escaped from the thieves in the crowded marketplace. Later on, however, the leader saw the brothers going into their house.

"Tonight, when they are asleep, we will come and capture them," said the leader of the thieves. He marked the door with chalk, so the thieves would find it that night.

Luckily, Kassim's clever servant girl, Morgiana, had seen the leader mark the door. She went to Ali Baba and told him. "I have a plan," said Morgiana. She went around all the local houses and marked the doors with chalk. That night, the forty thieves looked for the house, but it was impossible to find the right one.

The cunning thieves kept watch that day and the leader spotted Ali Baba leaving his house. This time, the leader made a chip in the front doorstep. However, he hadn't counted on clever Morgiana. She saw him make the chip and went around all the local houses, chipping their doorsteps, too. That night, the forty thieves couldn't find the house again.

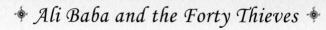

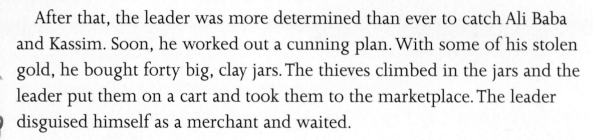

After that, the leader was more determined than ever to catch Ali Baba and Kassim. Soon, he worked out a cunning plan. With some of his stolen gold, he bought forty big, clay jars. The thieves climbed in the jars and the leader put them on a cart and took them to the marketplace. The leader disguised himself as a merchant and waited.

Soon, Ali Baba walked through the marketplace. "Kind sir," called the leader. "I have forty jars of olive oil that need to be stored. If you will put them in your house for one night, I will give you a gold coin."

"Of course," said Ali Baba. The leader took the jars into Ali Baba's house and when Ali Baba was gone, he climbed into the last empty one. The thieves planned to jump out of the jars and capture Ali Baba and Kassim that same night.

Once again, Morgiana was too clever for them. "The thieves are in the jars," she told Ali Baba. So, Ali Baba, Kassim and Morgiana tied up the lids of the jars, so they couldn't be opened. Then they carefully loaded the jars onto a cart and drove out of the city.

The thieves knew that they were moving. They shouted and struggled to get out of the jars, but they were trapped inside. Ali Baba drove the cart to the top of a big hill. Ali Baba, Kassim and Morgiana pushed the jars down the steep slope.

The jars rolled and rolled, all the way down the hillside and cracked at the bottom. The thieves were so frightened that they ran off and were never seen again.

Now, Ali Baba and Kassim were free to take all the treasure they wanted from the magic cave. In admiration at Morgiana's cleverness, Ali Baba married her and they lived happily ever after.

The Firebird

Once, there was a king who had three sons and an orchard full of magic trees. The trees grew apples made of pure gold. One night, as the king looked down from his castle at the orchard, he saw a bright firebird swoop down from the sky. It took a golden apple in its beak and flew away.

The king was very angry. The next night, he told his eldest son to stay in the orchard to catch the firebird. But the king's eldest son was very lazy. He fell asleep and didn't see the firebird return that night to steal another golden apple.

The next night, the king told his second son to stay in the orchard. However, the second son was even lazier than the eldest. He slept in the orchard all night and in the morning, another golden apple was gone.

The king's youngest son was called Ivan. He was determined to catch the firebird and went to the orchard. Ivan managed to stay awake long into the night and, when everything was quiet, he saw the firebird come down from the sky. Ivan tried to catch it, but he only grabbed a feather from its tail before it flew away.

When Ivan gave the feather to the king the next day, the king said "I must have the firebird. Whoever brings it to me will rule the land after me." So, the three brothers set out on horseback to find the firebird. They reached the edge of a dark, dangerous-looking wood.

"We're not going in there," said Ivan's two elder brothers. "We'll stay here and tell the king that the firebird was impossible to find."

But Ivan wasn't afraid, like his brothers. He rode his horse into the dark wood. Before long, he heard a growling sound. A big, grey wolf jumped out of the bushes. Ivan's horse threw him off and galloped away. "Now what will I do?" said Ivan to himself. "I'm stuck in this wood with no way of getting out. I'll never find the firebird now."

The big, grey wolf heard his words. "I'm sorry I frightened your horse," he said. "I have magic powers and I will take you to the firebird."

So, Ivan got on the wolf's back. The wolf carried him through the forest, far faster than any horse. When they stopped, they were by a big, red castle. "The firebird is in a golden cage, on the other side of the castle wall," said the wolf. "Take the firebird, but do not take its golden cage."

Ivan climbed over the castle wall and found the firebird. However, he couldn't resist taking the golden cage, too. Suddenly, loud bells began to sound. Guards surrounded Ivan and he was taken to the king of the red castle.

"You are a thief," said the king of the red castle. "The only way I will give you the firebird is if you fetch me the horse with the golden mane, that lives very far away from here."

Ivan left the castle and told the wolf what had happened. "I warned you not to take the cage," said the wolf. But the wolf carried Ivan a great distance, to another, even bigger castle. This castle was bright blue.
"Inside, is the horse with the golden mane," said the wolf. "But don't take its golden bridle."

Ivan sneaked into the blue castle and found the horse with the golden mane. Ivan got on the horse and rode away, but he forgot to take off its golden bridle. The bridle made a magical sound that woke everyone in the castle. Ivan was captured and taken before the king of the blue castle.

"You may have my horse if you can fetch me the most beautiful princess in the world," said the king of the blue castle.

Ivan told the wolf what had happened. "Don't say I didn't warn you," growled the wolf but, once again, it took Ivan an even greater distance, to a green castle, which was the biggest of them all.

The wall around the castle was too high for Ivan to climb. But the wolf leaped over it and soon leaped back with the princess and Ivan on its back. "Thank you for rescuing me," said the princess. "But I don't want to be taken to the king. I want to stay with you."

The wolf had a cunning plan. When they reached the blue castle, the wolf changed its shape, so it looked exactly like the princess. Ivan took the disguised wolf to the king, who was delighted.

The king gave Ivan the horse with the golden mane. The real princess and Ivan rode away to safety and waited for the wolf.

Meanwhile, the king of the blue castle tried to kiss his new princess. Just as he leaned forward, the wolf changed back into its real shape and the blue king found himself kissing a wolf! The king ran away, screaming with fright and the wolf bounded off, back to Ivan.

Soon, they all reached the red castle. "All I have to do is give the horse with the golden mane to the red king and he will give me the firebird," said Ivan.

But the horse with the golden mane didn't want to live with the king of the red castle and it neighed in fright. "It wants to stay with us," said the princess sadly.
"Leave this to me," said the wolf and it changed its shape until it looked exactly like the horse.

Ivan took the horse into the castle and exchanged it for the firebird. When Ivan and the princess had left, the king tried to ride the horse. The wolf turned back into its real shape and the king found himself riding a big, grey wolf! He fell off immediately and the wolf raced after Ivan.

Back at his father's castle, Ivan gave the firebird to his father, who was overjoyed. Ivan's two brothers were very jealous, but when they heard the wolf growl, they ran away in fright.

Ivan and the princess were soon married. The wolf and the horse with the golden mane stayed with them and they all lived happily ever after.

The Rabbit's Apprentice

Once, there was a very small boy, called Franz, who lived in a cottage next to a field full of rabbits. Franz never liked doing his chores. He grumbled when he had to clean his room. He grumbled when he had to eat all his dinner. Franz even grumbled when he had to get up in the morning.

Every afternoon, Franz used to sit at his window and watch the rabbits playing in the field. "It's very unfair," he thought. "Why should I have to clean my room, or eat food I don't like? The rabbits in the field don't have to do anything. They just play all the time."

One morning, Franz left his chores to go to the field where the rabbits lived. Suddenly, he heard a small voice. "Good day to you," it said. But there was nobody in the field except the rabbits. "I must be hearing things," thought Franz, then he saw a big rabbit nearby.

It was the big rabbit who had spoken. Franz had never met a talking rabbit before. "Good day," said Franz, in surprise.
"I am the king of the rabbits," said the big rabbit. "How are you?"

Franz told the king of the rabbits how miserable he was. "Come and live with us," said the rabbit king. "We have fun all day long."

The Rabbit's Apprentice

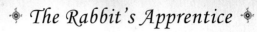

So Franz went away and made himself some rabbit ears out of paper. He tied them to his head and that evening, when the rabbits were out playing in the field, he jumped out of bed and went to join them.

"You can be my apprentice," said the king of the rabbits. "I will teach you all the ways of the rabbits. You can be one of us, now."

Franz had fun chasing around the field, but soon it was time for them to go to bed. "You can dig your own burrow tomorrow," said the rabbit king, "but for now, you are welcome to stay in my burrow."

Franz tried to fit into the burrow but, even though he was small, he could only just squeeze his body in and his head poked out of the ground. It wasn't very comfortable but, eventually, Franz drifted off to sleep.

After what seemed like no time at all, Franz was awoken by a rabbit. "Wake up, sleepyhead," it said. "You're missing all the fun."

It was so early in the morning, that it was still almost dark. Franz felt the king of the rabbits tickling his toes, so he climbed out of the burrow. Franz yawned. "Why are we awake so early?" he asked.
"We rabbits always wake up early," said the king. "Come on, there's a lot to do in the field."

The rabbits started digging holes in the ground. Franz started digging his new burrow with his hands, but the earth was very hard. Soon, he was dirty and tired and his hands hurt from all the digging.

All the other rabbits had dug deep holes, but the hole that Franz had dug was only a shallow pit in the ground. "I don't want to sleep there, tonight," thought Franz.

All the digging was making Franz very hungry. The rabbits were getting hungry, too. "Let's eat," said the king of the rabbits.
"Where do we get food from?" said Franz.
"It is all around us," said the king.

The rabbits all began to nibble grass from the field. Franz tried nibbling a bit of grass, too, but he spat it out straight away. It tasted awful.
"What about carrots?" said Franz. "Rabbits eat carrots."

"All the carrots are in the farmer's field," said one of the rabbits. "You can try to get some, if you like, but watch out for the farmer."

Franz was so hungry, he didn't care. He ran across to the farmer's field. He saw rows and rows of carrots in the ground, with only their feathery green leaves showing. Even though his hands were sore, Franz started to dig up some carrots. Just as he was ready to eat the carrots, the farmer appeared on the other side of a field.

"Hey, you," shouted the farmer. "Get off my land and stop stealing my carrots!" The farmer chased Franz all the way back to the rabbit field. Franz dived into the nearest burrow head first. The farmer marched back to his field of carrots, but when Franz climbed out of the burrow, he was completely covered in dirt.

Franz didn't want to be a rabbit anymore, so he went to see the king. "All I've done today is get up too early, dig horrible holes, eat horrible grass and get chased by a horrible farmer," compained Franz.

"That's what we do," said the king of the rabbits. "Isn't it fun?"
"No, it isn't," said Franz. "I'm afraid I'm going to have to stop being your apprentice, Your Majesty. I miss my old life. I want to have a nice warm bed to sleep in, real food to eat and a nice, long sleep at night."

The king of the rabbits smiled wisely. "I suppose things weren't really all that bad for you at home, then?" he said.
Franz had to agree. He thanked all the rabbits for having him to stay, said goodbye and went home, where his family were very happy to see him.

The next morning, Franz bounded out of bed, without any grumbling and he even cleaned his room. Franz' mother was so pleased with him, she asked him what he would like for dinner that night. "Anything but carrots!" said Franz with a big smile.

Hans and the Bears

Once upon a time, two big, wild bears lived in a forest. One day, when they were out looking for honey, they found a small bundle of fine clothes. Inside was a tiny baby, who was fast asleep.

"The child has been abandoned," said the brown, mother bear, patting the baby gently with her paw. "We should take him with us."
"We have children of our own," said the black, father bear, who was the biggest bear in the forest. "We cannot feed another."

However, when the baby started crying, even the black bear knew that they had to take care of him. So the bears took him home with them to their cave, deep in the woods, where their two bear cubs were waiting.

The child grew up with the bears, who named him Hans. He played roughly with his two bear brothers and learned to slap salmon out of the stream, climb trees in search of honey and sleep soundly all winter.

By the time he had grown into a young man, Hans was almost as strong as any bear. His only possession was a gold necklace that had been with him when he was found.

Hans was very clever and listened to the people that passed though the forest. He learned their language and he saw that they were like him. He even started to wear clothes like them. One day, Hans decided to leave the forest to live among humans.

"Take this acorn," said his bear brothers. "If you need help, crush it underfoot and we will be with you."

Hans said goodbye to his mother, the brown bear, who gave him a gigantic bear-hug. "Take this hazelnut," she said, wiping away her tears. "If you are in trouble, crush it underfoot and I will be with you."

Hans turned to his father, the great, black bear, who towered above him. "Take this walnut," said his father. "If you ever need help, crush it underfoot and I will be with you."

Hans said goodbye and set off on the road to the city. As night fell, Hans saw some other travellers up ahead. "Hello!" he cried. "Do you know a place where I can sleep?"

But the travellers were thieves. They pushed Hans to the ground and stole his necklace. Hans tried to use his great strength to fight them off, but they were too strong.

Hans took out the acorn and crushed it under his foot. Within moments, his two bear brothers were there. They fought off the thieves and returned the necklace to Hans. "Thank you, brothers," said Hans and continued on his way.

When Hans got to the city, he found that it was a confusing place. It was nothing like the quiet forest. Everyone was busy and nobody would stop to speak to him.

"I must get a job," thought Hans, but he didn't know how. He knocked on many doors, but found no work. Then, a mean-looking, old man saw Hans and stopped him in the street. "I have work in my show," he said.

Hans followed the old man to a crowded room where a thin-looking bear was chained to a post. The old man threw stones at the bear to make it dance, which made the crowd laugh and clap.

"This bear is very valuable to me," said the old man. "The king's chancellor is going to cut down the forest soon, so there will be no more bears in the kingdom. This will be the only one."

Hans was furious. He could not stand to see a bear treated so cruelly and he crushed the hazelnut. His mother appeared instantly. She sent the crowd running in fear. The old man's helpers tried to fight her off, but they were no match for her.

Hans unchained the poor, thin bear. It thanked him and ran off with the brown bear, back to the forest. Suddenly, the king's guard rushed in and surrounded Hans. "This is the ruffian who destroyed my bear show," shouted the old man. "I demand that he be taken to the king and executed."

Hans was brought in front of the king and queen in their castle, but it was their stern-looking chancellor who judged him. "For destroying the show, you are sentenced to death," said the chancellor. "Tomorrow, we will chop off your head!"

The guards didn't know how strong Hans was. He struggled free of them, took the walnut from his pocket, threw it to the floor and crushed it under his foot.

Soon, there was a roaring sound. It was the great, black bear, knocking the king's soldiers out of his way, in his haste to reach Hans. The bear burst into the room and was about to attack the guards, when the king cried out and pointed to Hans' golden necklace.

"Do not hurt the man, or the bear," commanded the king. Everyone stood still and waited for the king to speak. "We lost our son when we were attacked in the forest," said the king, in amazement. "We thought we would never see him again."

The king told how he had given his baby son a gold necklace, made by the royal jeweller, to celebrate his birth. "No other child has a necklace like that one," he said, looking at Hans. You must be our long-lost son and our kingdom is yours."

The king's chancellor was enraged because he had hoped to become king one day. He rushed at Hans with a dagger, but the black bear jumped at him and pushed him out of the castle window.

The chancellor landed with a splash in the castle moat. He climbed out, spluttering and ran far from the castle, never to be seen again.

Hans became a prince and he used his power to make sure that the bears' forest was left untouched. So Hans and the bears lived happily ever after.

The Enchanted Fiddle

Once, there was a poor boy named Peter, who often had very little to eat. He spent his days begging in the streets for crusts of bread. One hungry day, Peter wandered into the woods, looking for nuts and berries to fill his rumbling stomach.

Peter found a winding path he had never been down before. At the end of the path stood a strange cottage that was built under the roots of an old oak tree.

Peter looked inside the cottage and saw an old fiddle, lying in a case on a wooden table. The fiddle was a strange, shiny green. Peter looked around the old, dusty cottage. "Nobody has lived here for a long time," said Peter to himself. "They must have left this fiddle here and forgotten all about it. If I take it, I'm sure nobody will mind."

Even though he knew it was wrong, Peter took the fiddle. "I will sell this in the town and have enough to eat tonight," he thought. But he quickly ran from the strange little cottage, just in case.

However, when Peter got to the town, nobody seemed interested in buying the fiddle. "Who would want an odd, green fiddle like that?" the shopkeepers told him. "It looks like junk."

So, Peter didn't get any food that night. He sat down in the town square as the sun went down, hungrier than ever. He picked up the bow from the fiddle's case and moved it over the strings of the fiddle.

All at once, the air was filled with the loveliest music Peter had ever heard. His head filled with thoughts of delicious food. It was better than eating. As soon as he stopped playing, the thoughts disappeared.

Peter saw that a crowd had formed around him. "Play again!" said the people. Everyone who heard the music saw their hearts' desire. Peter played long into the night and some people gave him pennies for his playing, so he could afford something to eat.

That night, an old man came up to him when he had stopped playing. "That must be the fiddle that belongs to the wizard of the woods," said the man, looking at Peter with his sharp, old eyes. "You should take it back to him."

"I don't know what you mean," said Peter. "This is my fiddle."

The old man walked away without saying another word.

Soon, Peter was no longer poor. Everyone came to hear his music and they all gave him money. But the more Peter played, the unhappier he got. He knew that it was the fiddle that played the magic music, not him.

One night, the old man approached him again. "Why haven't you returned the fiddle? The wizard of the wood is waiting."

"Go away, old man," said Peter. "The fiddle is mine!"

Not long after, Peter was asked to go to the palace and play for the king. The king loved the music that Peter played. "I command you to stay here and be my royal musician," said the king.

But Peter shook his head. "I'm sorry, Your Majesty, but I must return the fiddle to its true owner."

So, Peter journeyed back into the forest where he had found the fiddle and searched for days for the strange cottage. But, try as he might, he couldn't find it. Pete was about to give up, when he heard a noise. Two ogres were lumbering through the forest. "Did you hear? The wizard of the woods has lost his magic fiddle," said one of the ogres. "His power is weak without it. Let's go and destroy his cottage."

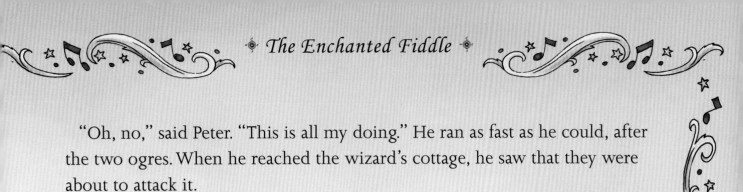

"Oh, no," said Peter. "This is all my doing." He ran as fast as he could, after the two ogres. When he reached the wizard's cottage, he saw that they were about to attack it.

The wizard of the woods was standing outside his cottage. He was a tall, old man with a long, grey beard and flowing robes. He was throwing weak bolts of magic at the ogres, but it was no use. The ogres both had huge, wooden clubs. They were laughing and using the clubs to hit the cottage until its walls trembled. "If only I had my magic fiddle!" cried the wizard.

Peter ran past the ogres, as fast as he could. He passed the fiddle to the wizard, who smiled at him. "Thank you, young sir," said the wizard. He put the fiddle to his chin and began to play.

This tune was nothing like the ones Peter could play. It was faster and louder. Peter could feel the wizard's magic all around him. Suddenly, the two ogres started dancing and they couldn't stop. They danced themselves away, far into the forest and never troubled the wizard again.

"That's better," said the wizard. He put down the fiddle and looked at Peter. For the first time, Peter recognised the wizard. It was the old man who he had met in town. "I'm sorry I stole your fiddle, sir," said Peter.

The wizard looked at Peter with his sharp, old eyes. "You came back to return it to me and you helped to save me from the ogres. So, I forgive you. However, there is one thing you must do. You must become my servant." Peter was very relieved that the wizard had forgiven him and he agreed to be his servant.

From that day on, Peter worked hard for the wizard. He learned lots of new things. However, Peter made sure that he never played the magic fiddle again.

The wizard looked after Peter, so he never went hungry and always had delicious food to eat. The two of them lived happily ever after, in the strange, old cottage that was built into the roots of an old oak tree.

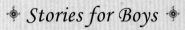

The Boy who Cried Wolf

Once upon a time, there lived a young shepherd boy. Every day, he took his sheep up the side of a mountain and let them graze. Every night, he took the sheep back down to their pen in the farm. All day long, the shepherd boy watched the sheep. It was very dull. "I wish I had some other people up here with me," he thought. "But nobody wants to walk all the way up the mountain, just to see me."

So, the shepherd boy ran down the mountain to where his older brother was farming the land, with several big farm workers helping him. "Help, a wolf is attacking my sheep!" cried the shepherd boy, jumping around and waving his hands.

At once, his brother and the farm workers rushed all the way up the mountain, puffing and panting. "Where's the wolf?" they cried. "There's no wolf," admitted the shepherd boy. "It was just a joke."

His brother and the farmhands went back down the mountain, in a very bad mood. The shepherd boy just giggled. "That was fun," he thought.

The next day, the shepherd boy decided to try his trick again. This time, he ran all the way down into the small village by the farm.

"Help, a wolf is attacking my sheep!" he cried. "Come, quickly." All the people in the village followed the shepherd boy up the hill.

"Ha, ha, there's no wolf," said the shepherd boy, when the people from the village reached the sheep. "It was just a trick." The shepherd boy rolled around on the grass, laughing, while the villagers left, angrily.

The next day, the shepherd boy decided to try his trick on an old shepherd who lived on the other side of the mountain. He ran round to the shepherd and cried, "Help, a wolf is attacking my sheep!"

The old shepherd looked hard at him, until the shepherd boy had to look away. "You're lying," said the old shepherd. "Now leave, before I set my sheepdog on you!"

The shepherd boy ran away, annoyed that his trick hadn't worked.

The next day, the shepherd boy saw a big, grey shape slinking behind his sheep. It was a wolf.

Quick as a flash, the shepherd boy ran down the mountain to the farm. "Wolf! Wolf!" he yelled. "There's a wolf on the mountain."
His brother and his brother's friends laughed at him. "We're not going to fall for that one again," his brother said.

So, the shepherd boy dashed into the village. "Please, help me!" he cried. "A real wolf is attacking the sheep."
"Go away," said the people of the village. "We don't have time to listen to your lies."

In despair, the shepherd boy ran back up the mountain. He saw that the wolf was sneaking closer and closer to the sheep.

The shepherd boy ran round the mountain to where the old shepherd sat with his sheepdog. "I know you won't believe me!" cried the shepherd boy, "but a real wolf is about to attack my sheep!"

The old shepherd stared hard at the shepherd boy and the shepherd boy thought he was going to send him away again. "Come on, then, boy," said the old shepherd, grimly. "There's not a moment to lose." They ran back round the mountain with the old shepherd's sheepdog.

When the sheepdog saw the wolf, it ran at it, growling. The wolf jumped back in surprise and then ran off, its tail between its legs.

After thanking the old shepherd, the shepherd boy went down into the village. He told everyone what had happened. "I'm sorry I lied to you all," said the shepherd boy, sadly. "I don't blame you for not believing me when I said a wolf was attacking my sheep. I'll never lie again."

Soon after, the old shepherd called the shepherd boy around to his side of the mountain. In the old shepherd's hut, the sheepdog had had six tiny puppies. "Take one," said the old shepherd. "It'll help you guard the sheep."

The shepherd boy chose a black and white puppy. It grew up to be a loyal sheepdog and together, the shepherd boy and his dog guarded the sheep well.

After that, the shepherd boy was never lonely. He didn't tell any more lies and he never cried, 'Wolf,' again.

The Fox and the Wolf

Once upon a time, a clever fox lived in a house with his wife and two cubs. The fox was friends with a fierce wolf. One day, the fox and the wolf decided to steal a joint of meat that was sitting in a farmer's kitchen. "You get it and throw it to me," said the fox. "I'll leave half for you."

The wolf climbed through the farmhouse window and threw the meat out to the fox. But the farmer saw the wolf and chased it all around the house, until the wolf managed to escape out of the window.

When the wolf found the fox in the forest, he saw that the fox had eaten all the meat off the bone. "Here," said the fox, I saved you half – the half that is made of bone!"
"You thief!" cried the wolf. "Tomorrow, I'll come to your den and make you pay for this."

The fox was very afraid. He worried that the angry wolf might come and gobble up him and his family. All night, he paced up and down, wondering what to do. Suddenly, he had an idea. "I'll wear a disguise and trick the wolf," he said.

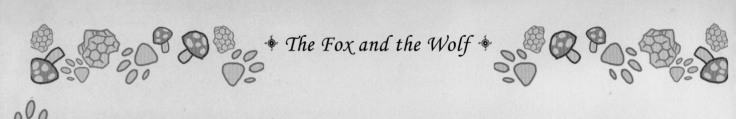

The next day, the fox put on his wife's best slippers and bonnet. He sipped tea with her in the wood. The angry wolf soon arrived. "Where is the fox?" he growled. "I'm going to teach him a lesson."
"This is my sister," said the fox's wife. "The fox is away today."

The fox felt very afraid, but he put on his highest voice. "A pleasure to meet you, Mister Wolf," he said.

"I'll be back again tomorrow," the wolf said. "Tell your husband to watch out!" The wolf left the den and the fox breathed a sigh of relief.
"What will you do tomorrow when the wolf returns?" asked the fox's wife, but the fox already had a plan.

The next day, the fox told one of his two cubs to hide in an old tree trunk, far from his den. "When you see the wolf, come out of your hiding place," said the fox.

Not long after this, the wolf returned to the fox's den. "Now it's time for my revenge, fox," said the wolf.
"Hello, wolf," said the fox. "We were just talking about you. My only child here says he can run faster than you."
The wolf snorted. "Impossible," he said.

 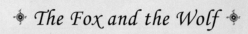
"Would you care for a bet?" asked the fox. "If my fox cub can reach the old, tree stump before you can, you must leave me alone today."
The wolf agreed and he raced off to the tree stump, as fast as he could.

When the wolf got to the stump, the fox's other cub came out. "I don't believe it," said the wolf. "This little cub has beaten me. I'll leave now, but I'll be back tomorrow."

The next day, the fox thought harder than ever, until he thought of a plan to make the wolf leave the forest for good. He searched the forest until he found a bees' nest, dripping with honey. The fox took the nest home, making sure that it dripped honey all through the forest, in a long trail.

 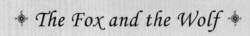 

The fox's house had a back door, as well as a front one. The fox made the honey trail go all the way to the back door, then he smeared honey all over the hallway.

Just then, the wolf arrived. "You'd better get out of here, wolf," said the fox. "My friend, the bear, is coming in through the back door soon. He said that if you touch me, he'll eat you up in one gulp."

The wolf didn't believe the fox "The bear is no friend of yours," he said. "Oh, really?" said the fox. "Go to my back door and see." So, the wolf went to the back door, getting honey all over his paws and fur.

Meanwhile, the old bear who lived in the forest had found the fox's honey trail. It followed it all through the forest, licking up the honey. When it got to the fox's back door, it stuck its great, brown head through.

The wolf saw the bear and yelped with fright. The bear could smell the honey on the wolf and wanted to lick it off. But the wolf turned to run. "Come back," called the bear, in its growling voice. "I'm still hungry!"

The wolf was so frightened that it ran out the fox's front door, whining and howling. It ran and ran until he was far away from the forest and never returned. So, the fox, the fox's wife and their two little cubs, lived happily ever after.

Sinbad and the Giant

Once upon a time, there was a fearless sailor named Sinbad. Sinbad and his brave crew sailed the seven seas, exploring strange, new lands and always looking for rare and exotic goods to trade. Often, their searches led them into dangerous adventures, but none was as deadly as Sinbad's encounter with the one-eyed giant.

Sinbad was sailing back to his home, with a ship laden with treasure, when a mighty storm blew up. Huge waves rose higher than the mast and crashed down on the deck. Thunder rattled above the ship and lightning blasted down to strike the mast. Sinbad and his men were thrown into the sea. When the storm cleared, the sailors found themselves washed up on a deserted island. There was no sign of their ship.

The crew explored the island, but the only animals they could find were a herd of sheep grazing on a grassy hill. As Sinbad climbed the hill, he saw a mighty fortress on the other side. Its great doors were open, so Sinbad and his men stumbled inside. There they found an empty courtyard. It was lined with tall doors, all of which were closed. Sinbad and his men were exhausted. They soon fell asleep in the courtyard.

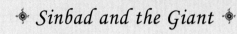
The sailors woke up to a thundering sound so loud, they thought the storm had returned. But it was not the storm. A flock of sheep had run into the courtyard. They were followed by a mighty giant. It was his footsteps that were making so much noise. The giant was as tall as four men standing on each others' shoulders. He was fierce and foul-smelling and he had a single eye in the middle of his forehead.

The men tried to escape, but the giant had closed the great doors behind them. "What's this?" roared the giant. "I can smell human beings!" The giant peered at them with his huge eye. Sinbad noticed that the giant couldn't see very well. However, the giant managed to grab Sinbad. "You're very skinny," said the giant, throwing Sinbad to the ground. He picked up another man and felt him all over. "Another skinny one," he said, grumpily, throwing the sailor down.

The ship's cook was a much fatter man. He tried to run from the giant, but the giant scooped him up easily. "That's more like it," bellowed the giant. "Tomorrow night, I will make a big fire and roast you for my dinner!" The giant opened one of the big doors and went into his castle, leaving Sinbad and his men trapped in the gloomy courtyard.

The poor cook was terrified that he was going to be eaten. "Don't worry," said Sinbad. "When the giant lets his sheep out tomorrow morning, we'll rush out, too." So, the next morning, when the giant opened his gates to let the sheep out, Sinbad and his men tried to leave. But the giant saw them and slammed the heavy gate shut before they could get out.

That night, when the giant came back in, he made a fire and tried to find the cook. But Sinbad was too clever for the giant. He hid the fat cook in a pile of sheepskins that were lying in a corner of the courtyard. Then he marched up to the giant. "Look what you've done to me," said Sinbad, trying to sound like the cook. "I'm so frightened, I've become nothing more than skin and bone."

The giant picked Sinbad up. "You're not worth eating," he said. He threw Sinbad and his men some mutton, which they ate, hungrily. "I'll fatten you up, then eat you tomorrow night," said the giant, going to bed inside his castle.

"How will we get out?" asked the fat cook, coming out from under the sheepskins. Sinbad looked at the sheepskins. "I think I have a plan," he said.

The next morning, when the giant went to let his sheep out, he found that Sinbad and his crew had built a big, smoky fire. The giant could hardly see anything. "You're not getting out," he yelled. As he let his sheep out, he felt along each one's back, to make sure it wasn't Sinbad, or his men. "That's funny," said the giant. "I have more sheep than I thought."

The giant didn't realise that Sinbad and his crew had put sheepskins over their backs and walked out on all fours, pretending to be sheep.

Sinbad and his men ran to the other side of the island and chopped down some trees to make big rafts. By evening, they were almost ready to sail.

However, when the giant herded his sheep back to his castle that night, he realised that the men were gone. "I've been tricked!" he boomed and Sinbad could hear it from the other side of the island.

The giant stomped all over the island, looking all around with his one, giant eye. As Sinbad tied the last of the logs to the raft, he made sure everyone was on it. "Set sail!" he cried and the men raised the sheepskin sails.

Just as they were pushing off the raft, the giant saw them. He waded right into the sea. The sailors paddled as fast as they could, but the wind kept blowing them backwards. The giant was up to his neck in the ocean, but he raised his huge hands and tried to smash the raft.

"Cut down the mast," cried Sinbad. The sailors were amazed, but they did what they were told. The tall mast of the raft toppled over and struck the angry giant on the head. The giant sunk right to the bottom of the ocean and never troubled anybody again.

"Now we are stuck in the sea without a mast," said the fat cook, sadly. "We'll never get home."
"There's something on the horizon," said one of the men. "It's our ship!"

Sure enough, Sinbad's ship had survived the storm. Sinbad and his men sailed back home with all their treasure and a wonderful story of a one-eyed giant to tell.

Sinbad and the Giant

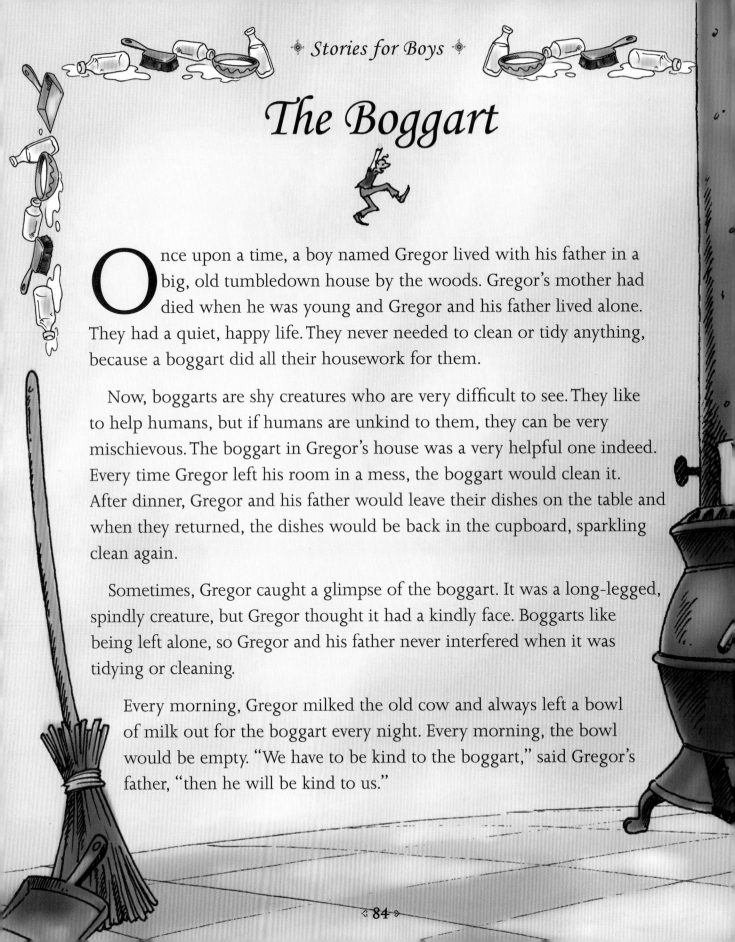

The Boggart

Once upon a time, a boy named Gregor lived with his father in a big, old tumbledown house by the woods. Gregor's mother had died when he was young and Gregor and his father lived alone. They had a quiet, happy life. They never needed to clean or tidy anything, because a boggart did all their housework for them.

Now, boggarts are shy creatures who are very difficult to see. They like to help humans, but if humans are unkind to them, they can be very mischievous. The boggart in Gregor's house was a very helpful one indeed. Every time Gregor left his room in a mess, the boggart would clean it. After dinner, Gregor and his father would leave their dishes on the table and when they returned, the dishes would be back in the cupboard, sparkling clean again.

Sometimes, Gregor caught a glimpse of the boggart. It was a long-legged, spindly creature, but Gregor thought it had a kindly face. Boggarts like being left alone, so Gregor and his father never interfered when it was tidying or cleaning.

Every morning, Gregor milked the old cow and always left a bowl of milk out for the boggart every night. Every morning, the bowl would be empty. "We have to be kind to the boggart," said Gregor's father, "then he will be kind to us."

Time passed and eventually Gregor's father married again. His new wife moved into the house and became Gregor's stepmother. "Treat your new mother well," Gregor's father told him. But Gregor didn't like his new stepmother. She was proud, cold and spiteful.

When Gregor's father was out working, she would tease Gregor. "You've become lazy because of that boggart," she said. "You should be doing all the chores around here, instead of that filthy creature."

One night, when Gregor was about to pour the milk out for the boggart, his stepmother stopped him. "What a stupid waste," she said. "The boggart doesn't need our food. I'm sure it can find its own meals."

Gregor protested, but his stepmother was firm. That night, Gregor went to sleep, wondering what would happen when the boggart saw it didn't have any milk. Would it be angry?

The next day, Gregor came downstairs to find that nothing had been tidied away. So, Gregor's stepmother set him to work doing all the chores. By the end of the day, Gregor was exhausted.

The next morning, Gregor came down to find that all the plates had been taken out of the cupboard and piled on the table. "Stupid boy," said his stepmother. "Why did you do that?"
"I didn't," said Gregor. "It was the boggart. You're making him angry!"
"Nonsense," said his stepmother. "Now put those plates away and dust the yard."

The boggart must have really missed its milk. The next day, Gregor came downstairs to find that all the furniture in the house had been turned upside down!

Day after day, the boggart kept on moving things around and even leaving big, muddy footprints all around the house. Gregor had to clear it all up, which he thought was very unfair. He was as angry with his stepmother as the boggart was.

The boggart became more and more mischievous. When Gregor's father went to sit down, his chair would be yanked away from behind him. Buckets of water were perched on top of doors, to fall on whoever opened them. The boggart made the clocks run backwards and scared the cow, so that its milk turned sour.

When his stepmother wasn't watching him, Gregor ran to an old, wise woman who lived in a tiny cottage, in a nearby valley, to ask what he should do. "A mistreated boggart is a terrible thing," said the old woman. "To see the boggart and guard against its mischief, you'll need a stone with a hole in it. Look through the stone and you'll see the boggart. Speak through the stone and you may be able to calm him down."

Gregor went out into the fields and found a stone with a hole in it. Gregor took it back home, but things had gone from bad to worse. Gregor's stepmother was standing in the kitchen and all the pots, pans and plates were flying around her head. She used a frying pan to bat them away.

Gregor tried not to laugh. He looked through the hole in the stone and clearly saw the boggart leaping around, throwing plates and looking very angry.

Gregor spoke softly to the boggart, just as the old woman had told him to do. However, the boggart would not calm down. He seemed to become even angrier and flung even more things at the stepmother.

"I'm sorry I mistreated you, Gregor," said his stepmother, who was very frightened. "I promise to be good from now on, if only you'll save me from the boggart!"

That night, Gregor left milk out for the boggart. He took the stone and looked through it. But Gregor had forgotten that boggarts like to be left alone."

Suddenly, the creature noticed that he was being stared at. Gregor thought for a moment that he was going to start throwing things at him. However, he jumped up and down shaking his fists.

The boggart was very upset and ran away. Gregor looked through the stone and saw the long-legged boggart dancing away, over the hills. "No milk was one thing – being looked at is another," said the boggart. "I'm off to find another family. Goodbye, Gregor."

From that day on, Gregor never saw the boggart again. But his stepmother was much nicer to him. Gregor, his stepmother and his father all took turns to do the chores and lived happily ever after.

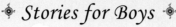

Dick Whittington and His Cat

Once upon a time, there was a poor boy named Dick Whittington. Dick's parents had died when he was very little, so he was very poor and alone.

One day, as he was begging for food, Dick heard two villagers talking. "The streets of London are paved with gold," said one to the other.

Dick decided to go to London. "If the streets are paved with gold, I will make my fortune there," he thought.

Dick travelled for many days, until he reached London. However, the streets of London weren't paved with gold. Everything was noisy, dirty and smelly and there was no work anywhere.

Dick was very tired and hungry. He rested on the doorstep of a grand house. He woke to find a grumpy cook staring at him. "Be off with you!" she cried. "We'll have no tramps here."

"Wait," said a kindly voice. It was the master of the house. "What's the matter, boy?"
Dick told the master that he was looking for work and had no food.

The man, whose name was Mr Fitzwarren, gave Dick a job, working in his kitchen. Dick was very happy and decided to work as hard as he could. Mr Fitzwarren's daughter, Alice, took pity on him, and gave him scraps of fine food from her meals.

However, life was still very hard for Dick. The cook treated him badly and made him do all the hardest work. His little room in the loft of the house was filled with rats and mice, which scampered over his bed at night, so he could never get to sleep.

Early one morning, in an alley outside the house, Dick saw a cold, thin and hungry-looking kitten. Taking pity on it, he gave her some of his food. The kitten purred and jumped into his arms. From that moment, the kitten followed Dick everywhere. She grew up to be a sleek and elegant cat. Every night, the cat would come up to Dick's room and chase away all the rats and mice.

Mr Fitzwarren was a rich merchant who sent ships across the sea to far-off lands. The ships were full of things to sell and when they returned, they were always full of gold. Everyone in Mr Fitzwarren's house was allowed to put something on the ship to sell far away, to see if it would bring them money. Only Dick had nothing to put on the ship.

"Why not put your cat on board?" said Alice to Dick. "Someone may want to buy her."
Dick was sad to see his cat go, but he put her on board Mr Fitzwarren's ship before it sailed away.

From that day on, Dick was lonelier than ever. The cook treated him even worse than before and now there was no cat to keep away the rats and mice.

One day, Dick could stand it no longer. He gathered up his few belongings and decided to return to the village where he was born.
"London is too hard a place for me," he thought, sadly, as he crossed the hills that led away from the city. Just then, the bells of the great church at Bow began to peal. Dick stopped. "Turn again, Whittington, Lord Mayor of London," they seemed to be saying.

"Could I really be Lord Mayor, one day?" said Dick, turning back towards the city. "Then I will stay in London." He ran back down the hill and was back at Mr Fitzwarren's house, before anyone even knew he had left.

Meanwhile, Dick's little cat was travelling across the sea in the big ship. The ship was filled with rats and mice that nibbled at all the food in the ship's kitchen. The cat guarded the food, so the rats and mice could not get it.

The crew fed her well in thanks. "That cat is the best mouser we've ever seen," they said.

Months passed and the ship crossed the waves and reached a far-off land. A great and powerful queen lived there, but her palace was overrun with rats.

When the crew sat to eat with the queen, hundreds of rats dashed out of holes, scampered onto the table, and ate all the food. "I wish there was something that would stop these creatures," said the queen.

One of the crew remembered Dick's cat, who was asleep on board the ship. He fetched the cat and brought it to the queen.

As soon as the cat saw the rats, it leapt onto the table and chased them all away. The rats were so terrified that they hurried out of the palace and never came back.

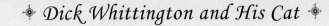

The queen was delighted. "I will give the owner of this cat a thousand pieces of gold!" she said. She then gave the cat a collar made of solid gold and returned it to the ship. When the ship sailed back to London, Mr Fitzwarren took the chest of gold to Dick, who was scrubbing the floors in the kitchen.

"Dick," said Mr Fitzwarren, "your cat has come back and she's earned you more money than I have ever seen!" Dick couldn't believe his eyes. With the chest of gold, he was suddenly the richest man in London. He generously gave gold pieces to all the people who had helped him while he was poor. He even gave some to the cook, who stopped being quite so grumpy.

Now Dick was rich, he bought the finest house in London and eventually married Alice who had been so kind to him while he was poor. The words of Bow Bells came true as well. Dick Whittington became a prosperous merchant and when he was older, he became Lord Mayor of London. However, he never forgot that it was all thanks to his little cat.

The Brave Little Donkey

Once, there was a little donkey who lived with his mother in a field. The little donkey was very happy. All day long he would play and eat juicy, green grass.

However, the little donkey soon grew bigger and the time came for him to be sold so that he could go and work somewhere else.

"You must work hard," said the little donkey's mother. "Just remember that you will always have the the three donkey gifts — your bite, your kick and your loud bray."

The donkey was sold to a farmer who lived in a farmhouse with his large family. The donkey loved his new life. He slept in a warm stable, next to the house. The children of the family loved riding the donkey around the farmyard and he was so much a part of the family, he was even allowed inside the farmhouse. Sometimes, late at night, the children would poke a bunch of carrots through the stable door for him to eat.

A band of robbers moved to the area, looking for things to steal. When they saw the farmhouse, they decided to creep in and steal everything they could find.

The easiest way into the farmhouse was through the stables. That night, one of the robbers made a hole in the stable door and reached his hand through to unlock it.

The Brave Little Donkey

The donkey was sleeping in the stables when it saw the robber's hand poking through the door in the dark. The donkey thought it was a bunch of carrots. He reached over to the hand and bit down hard. The robber ran off in pain and fright.

"The farmer must have a ferocious guard dog," said the robber to his friends. "Look at this bite on my hand. We will have to find a different way in."

The next night, the robbers tried to rob the farmhouse again. The donkey heard a noise and looked out of the stable. He saw the robbers trying to break open the front door of the farmhouse.

The donkey began to bray. It was a very loud sound and made the robbers run away immediately. However, by the time the farmer and his family had come downstairs and out to the stables, the robbers were long gone.

"Why do you make so much noise, donkey?" said the farmer. "You've woken us all up." The farmer was very angry with the donkey, but the donkey knew he had saved the family.

The next day, the donkey was allowed into the kitchen while a great feast was being prepared for a party that night. The donkey was very hungry, because the children had forgotten to feed him that day. When everyone was out, he decided to taste one of the cakes that had been left out.

The donkey ate another cake and then another one after that. He even ate the vegetables, the roast beef, the bread and the cheese.

By the time the family came back, all the food was gone and the donkey was standing in the middle of a messy, empty kitchen.

The farmer was furious. "Get out," he said to the donkey. "There'll be no cosy stable for you tonight. As punishment, you'll sleep in the barn."

The donkey was very sorry for what it had done. The barn that night was very cold. It was stacked with big logs and there was hardly enough room to lie down.

The donkey shivered and stuck his head through the window of the barn. He saw the gang of robbers again. They were sneaking into the house through a different door. The donkey tried braying, but the farmer just shouted at him to be quiet.

"I've used my bite and my bray," thought the donkey. "Now it's time for my kick!" Quick as a flash, the donkey kicked the wide, barn doors open. Before the robbers could move, he stood behind the enormous pile of logs and gave them a big kick with his hind legs. The logs rolled out of the barn, onto the robbers, trapping them.

The farmer came downstairs and saw that the brave donkey had trapped the robbers. "Thank you," he said. "You've saved us."

As a reward, the farmer bought the donkey all the carrots he could eat. The children piled his stable with warm hay and the donkey never had to sleep in the cold barn again.

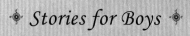

Aladdin

Long ago, in a great city, there lived a poor, hungry orphan boy named Aladdin. He had no home of his own, so he had to live on the streets and steal food to survive.

One day, a wealthy-looking man called to Aladdin in the marketplace. Aladdin thought the man was about to punish him for stealing and he tried to hide. "Don't be afraid," said the man. "I am your long-lost uncle, Abenazer. If you will help me, Aladdin, together we will make our fortune."

Aladdin didn't know that Abenazer was not really his uncle, but a wicked magician. Abenazer wanted a magic lamp that lay in an enchanted cave nearby, but he was cowardly and wanted Aladdin to get it for him.

Abenazer took Aladdin to the cave entrance, which was a small hole that led down a steep slope. "You may take all the treasure you find inside," said Abenazer. "Just bring me the dirty old lamp from the middle of the cave."

Aladdin went into the cave. He had never seen so much treasure. Gold was piled in heaps on the floor and the walls of the cave were covered with precious stones. Aladdin filled his pockets with jewels. He found a gold ring on the floor and put it on his finger.

Aladdin found the old lamp on a large stone in the middle of the cave. He took the lamp, but the moment it was in his hands, the floor started to shake. Aladdin looked up to find the entrance to the cave closing above him. Climbing as fast as he could, he reached the opening of the cave. "Help me out, Uncle," cried Aladdin.

"Give me the lamp first," said Abenazer. He tried to grab the lamp, but he knocked Aladdin, who was still holding it, down the rocky slope. Aladdin tumbled back down into the cave and when he looked up, the entrance to the cave had closed behind him.

Aladdin sat in the dark, wondering what to do. He was trapped in the cave. "That man was no uncle of mine," he said, rubbing the dirty lamp to clean it. "How I wish I had some light in here."

Suddenly, a mighty, green genie whooshed from the spout of the lamp. The genie made more lamps appear, so the cave was flooded with light.

"I am the genie of the lamp. My wish is your command. What is your next wish, Master?" said the genie.

Aladdin was amazed. "I wish I were at home," he said. The genie clicked his fingers and Aladdin was back in the marketplace, surrounded by the jewels he was carrying.

From then on, the genie appeared every time Aladdin rubbed the lamp. It could make all of Aladdin's wishes come true. "I wish for a great palace!" cried Aladdin. The ground shook and a mighty, marble palace rose from the desert. It was bigger than the palace of the sultan himself.

Soon, Aladdin was the richest man in the city. He married the sultan's daughter and they lived happily in their desert palace.

However, Abenazer had not forgotten Aladdin. When he found out that Aladdin had the lamp, he came up with a plan to get the lamp and use its power for himself.

Abenazer disguised himself as a poor lamp-seller. Then, he went to Aladdin's palace with a cart full of new lamps, "New lamps for old!" he cried.

Aladdin's wife didn't know that Aladdin's lamp was magical. She gave Abenazer the old magic lamp, in return for a shiny new one.

As soon as Abenazer had the lamp, he told the genie to take away all Aladdin's wealth and his palace. Abenazer made himself sultan and imprisoned Aladdin's wife. Aladdin was a poor man, once again.

All that Aladdin had left was the gold ring he had taken from the enchanted cave. "I must sell it to buy food," Aladdin thought. "But I don't know how I can get my wife and my palace back."

Aladdin cleaned the ring with an old rag and suddenly, a great, blue genie whooshed out of it. "I am the genie of the ring," said the genie. "What is your wish?"

Aladdin asked the genie of the ring to restore his power, but the genie could not. "The genie of the lamp is more powerful than me," explained the genie of the ring. "I cannot reverse his magic."

Aladdin asked the genie to take him to Abdenazer. In the blink of an eye, he was outside the sultan's palace. Through the windows, he could see that Abenazer had become Sultan.

Aladdin thought of a cunning plan to get his lamp back. "Genie of the ring," he said. "I wish for a potion that will send anyone who drinks it to sleep."
"Your wish is my command, Master," said the genie. It conjured up a bottle of the potion.

Aladdin sneaked into the palace, past Abenazer's guards and found his wife. He gave her the bottle of potion and told her his plan.

Aladdin went to hide and his wife called to Abenazer, "Let me out of this prison and I'll marry you."

Abenazer let Aladdin's wife out and she dropped the potion into his drink. Abenazer started to yawn and soon he was asleep, with the lamp under his arm.

When Aladdin was sure that Abenazer was asleep, he came out of his hiding place. He pulled the lamp from Abenazer's grasp and quickly rubbed it before Abenazer could awake. "Restore my palace and banish Abenazer forever!" cried Aladdin to the genie of the lamp.

In the blink of an eye, Aladdin and his wife were back in their own, splendid palace. The genie sent Abenazer, far, far away, to the other side of the world and Aladdin and his wife lived happily every after.

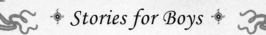

Jack and the Beanstalk

Once upon a time, a poor widow lived with her only son, Jack. He was an adventurous boy who was always getting into mischief, but he loved his mother dearly. Jack and his mother never had any money and their only possession was a black and white cow.

One day, there was no food left in the house and the cow wouldn't give any milk. "We shall have to sell the cow," said Jack's mother, sadly. "Take her to market tomorrow and get the best price you can for her."

The next day, Jack led the cow to the market. On the way, he met a strange-looking man. "That's a fine cow you have there," said the man. "Will you sell her to me for these beans? They are magic beans, as you will see."

"My mother will be cross," Jack thought to himself. But the magic beans sounded very exciting. So, he exchanged the cow for the beans and went home.

When Jack's mother heard what he had done, she was furious. "You sold our only possession for a handful of beans. Now we have nothing!" She threw the beans out of the window and sent Jack to bed.

The next morning, Jack woke up and looked out of his window. In the tiny garden, an enormous beanstalk had sprouted from the beans. It went so high up into the sky, its top disappeared into the clouds.

"They really were magic beans," said Jack, in amazement. "I wonder what's at the top of the beanstalk?"

Jack began to climb the beanstalk. He climbed and climbed until he was so high, he could see the countryside for miles around and his cottage looked no bigger than a dot.

Jack climbed even higher until he was above the clouds. He finally reached the top of the beanstalk and was surprised to find that he was in a whole new country. Everything was enormous. The daisies towered above him. The grass was like a forest. He even saw a beetle as big as a cat.

Jack saw a huge castle in the distance and went to explore it. He had just crept inside when suddenly, he heard a thumping sound. It was the footsteps of the giant who lived in the castle, returning home.

Jack sneaked inside a huge oven and watched. The giant was carrying three big bags of gold. Suddenly, he sniffed the air and bellowed,

"Fee, fi, fo, fum,
I smell the blood of an Englishman.
Be he alive, or be he dead,
I'll grind his bones to make my bread!"

The giant searched everywhere for Jack, but he didn't look in the oven.
Eventually, the giant sat at his kitchen table and fell asleep. Jack opened the
oven door and crept out. He grabbed one of the bags of money and sneaked
back to the beanstalk, then climbed down carefully. His mother was delighted
to see him and they had enough money to live on for many months.

However, eventually, the money ran out. "I must climb the beanstalk to the
castle again," said Jack and he climbed to the top of the beanstalk once more.
The giant was out again but, on his enormous kitchen table was a beautiful
hen. Jack was about to snatch it, when he heard the giant return.
The giant cried,

"Fee, fi, fo, fum,
I smell the blood of an Englishman.
Be he alive, or be he dead,
I'll grind his bones to make my bread!"

Jack hid in a giant mousehole, so the giant could not find him. The giant sat at the table and pulled out a little golden harp and started to play it. Suddenly, the hen laid an egg of pure gold. The giant leaned back on his chair in satisfaction and was soon fast asleep.

Jack came out of his hiding place, put the hen under his arm and crept out of the kitchen. Suddenly, the hen let out a loud squawk. The giant woke up with a start and saw that his hen was gone, but Jack was already charging back to the beanstalk.

At home, Jack tried to get the hen to lay a golden egg, but it just clucked, sadly. "We need the golden harp," said Jack. So he climbed the beanstalk one more time, until he was back in the land above the clouds. Searching through the giant's house, Jack found the harp in an enormous cupboard. Just as he was about to creep away with it, he heard the giant bellowing,

"Fee, fi, fo, fum,
I smell the blood of an Englishman.
Be he alive, or be he dead,
I'll grind his bones to make my bread!"

Jack grabbed the harp and ran out of the castle with it. However, the harp was magical and could speak. "I'm being stolen!" it cried out.

The giant thundered after Jack who ran as fast as he could, for fear that he would be caught and his bones ground up to make the giant's bread.

At last, Jack reached the beanstalk and climbed down. Behind him, the giant jumped onto the beanstalk and began climbing down, too.

◆ Jack and the Beanstalk ◆

At the bottom of the beanstalk, Jack fetched an axe. He chopped and chopped at the beanstalk with all his might until the beanstalk wobbled and tottered and crashed down. The giant fell to the ground and was so shocked, he ran away and never came back.

Jack and his mother played the magic harp to the hen and it began to lay golden eggs. With so much gold, Jack and his mother were never poor again and they lived happily ever after.

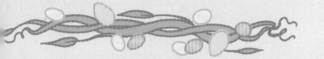

The Brave Little Tailor

Once upon a time, there lived a little tailor who liked to brag about even the smallest things he'd done.

One day, the tailor was about to eat some bread and jam when he saw that seven flies had settled on it. As quick as a flash, the tailor swatted them all away with one blow. "I must be the fastest fly-swatter in the world," said the tailor, proudly. "I want everyone to know how quick and clever I am."

The tailor took a belt and sewed the words SEVEN IN ONE BLOW into it. He wore the belt proudly, every day and even paraded round his village wearing it.

News of the tailor and his belt travelled through the village. "What do you think it means?" said the villagers to each other.
"Maybe it means he knocked down seven men in one blow," said one woman. Before long, everyone for miles around was telling the story of how the little tailor had beaten seven men with a single blow.

The story spread far and wide. It even reached the rocky wastes where the giants lived. It fell on the ears of one, very mean and nasty giant who had poor eyesight. "So this tailor knocked down seven men with one blow, eh?" the giant rumbled to himself. "I'm going to find him and see just how strong he is."

The giant travelled across the land in great strides. He was as tall as the church steeples he passed and all the people ran away in fear when they heard the thunder of his footsteps.

In no time at all, the giant reached the tailor's village. "Where is the man who beat seven in one blow?" he boomed.
The frightened villagers pointed to the tailor sitting on a nearby hill.
He was about to eat his lunch of bread and cheese.

The giant strode over to the tailor. When he saw how small the tailor was, he started to laugh. "Ha, ha, ha," he boomed. "When I heard you beat seven men with one blow, I came to challenge you to a fight. I'm going to squash you to a pulp," chuckled the giant.

The tailor was very scared. However, despite all his bragging, he really was rather brave and clever.

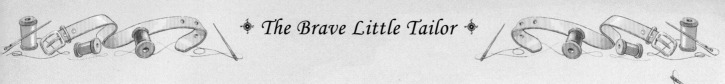

Trying to keep his voice from squeaking, the tailor called out, "It's true what you've heard, Master Giant. But I'm afraid, if we fought, I would really hurt you. To prove you're worthy of fighting me, let's have a contest of strength."

The giant agreed and picked up a big stone. He squeezed the stone as hard as he could, until the stone shattered in his hand. "Now it's your turn," said the giant. "If you're so strong, you shatter a stone!"

The tailor picked up the large, round cheese that he had been about to eat. It looked just like a big stone. "Is that all you can do?" the tailor said. "Any old giant can shatter a stone, but only I can get water out of one." He squeezed the cheese as hard as he could, until all the water ran out of it.

"I'm sure you can't throw a stone as far as I can!" roared the giant. He picked up a grey stone and hurled it into the air. The tailor watched as the stone soared high above them. It finally splashed into a lake, miles away.

Although the tailor was very scared, he looked around him for something to throw. He saw a grey wood-pigeon, asleep on the branch of a nearby tree. When the giant wasn't looking, the tailor picked up the pigeon and covered it with his hands.

"When I throw a stone," said the tailor, "it goes so high, it never comes down!" The tailor threw the pigeon high into the air. The pigeon quickly flew off into the distance.

The giant was amazed. "Maybe you are as strong as you claim." he said. "Let's camp on that hill, on the other side of the village. Uproot one of these trees and carry it over there and we'll make a fire."

Now the tailor was really scared. There was no way he could uproot a tree. However, he thought quickly. He went over to a clump of trees and started tying a rope around them. "What are you doing?" asked the giant.

"It's too easy to pick up one tree," said the tailor. "I was going to pick up all these trees in one go."
"But we only need one tree," said the giant.

"If we only need one, it's hardly worth bothering with," said the tailor. "You pull the tallest tree out and I'll help you carry it over to the hill."

The giant put his arms around the tallest tree and heaved with all his might. With a great creaking crunch, the tree came out of the ground.

"You take the root end and I'll take the heavier end with all the branches," shouted the tailor. While the giant was picking up the root end of the tree, the tailor climbed into its branches.

The giant picked up the huge tree and put it over his shoulder. Then he set off for the hill. But the tree was a very heavy one. The tailor kept calling out from the branches, "Come on, hurry up. I'm doing all the work." The giant looked around, but he couldn't see the tailor because the branches were in the way. Eventually, the giant had to give up. He put the tree down and lay on the ground, exhausted.

Meanwhile, the tailor jumped down from the tree. "Master Giant, I'm ready to fight you now," he said, jumping up and down and shaking his fists. The giant looked at the tailor in fear. He didn't seem tired at all. "You'll knock me down with one blow!" cried the giant and ran off in fright. He was so scared that he never came near the village again.

The villagers congratulated the brave little tailor on his cunning victory. They said that they would always feel safe as long as they had someone as strong and brave as the tailor to protect them.

The tailor didn't boast about it because he'd learned his lesson. After that, he never boasted again and everyone in the village lived happily ever after.

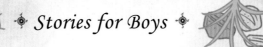

The Three
Billy Goats Gruff

Once upon a time, there were three goats who lived in a field high up in the mountains. They were named the Three Billy Goats Gruff and they loved to eat the fresh green grass in their meadow. But they ate so much of it that soon, there was hardly any left. The Billy Goats Gruff became thin and hungry.

One day, the Three Billy Goats Gruff saw a far-away meadow. It was full of young, fresh, green grass that looked delicious. But the meadow was on the other side of a rushing river. "How can we cross the river and reach the meadow?" asked the smallest Billy Goat Gruff.

"Look," said the middle-sized Billy Goat Gruff. "There is an old stone bridge across the river."

"I am going to cross the bridge and try that delicious grass," said the youngest Billy Goat Gruff.

"Wait," said the biggest Billy Goat Gruff, in his big deep voice. "Before you cross that bridge, there is something you should know. I have heard that a terrible troll lives under the bridge. He is big and hungry and has a long nose and horrible, sharp teeth."

The smallest Billy Goat Gruff didn't care about a silly old troll. "I may be small, but I am brave and bold," he said, in his little voice. "I'm not scared of any troll."
So the smallest Billy Goat Gruff skipped along to the bridge and started to cross it. His little hooves went *trip-trap, trip-trap* on the bridge.

Suddenly, a voice came from under the bridge. It was a snarling, slobbering, snickering kind of voice. "Who's that trip-trapping over my bridge?" it said.

It was the troll. He leapt out from under the bridge and cried, "I'm going to gobble you up for my dinner!" He sharpened his claws and got ready to leap on the smallest Billy Goat Gruff.

The little Billy Goat Gruff was frightened, but he thought quickly. Before the troll could leap on him, he cried, "Wait! Don't eat me! I am very thin and small. If you let me eat the grass on the other side of the bridge, I will grow big and fat. Then you can eat me when I come back."

The troll was hungry, but he was greedy, too and not very clever. "All right, little goat," said the troll. "I'll let you go, but make sure you're fattened up when you come back."

So, the smallest Billy Goat Gruff trip-trapped all the way across the bridge, to eat the tender green grass in the meadow.

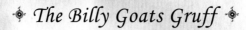

Soon, the middle-sized Billy Goat Gruff said to the biggest goat, "I am worried about our brother. I am going across the bridge to see if he is safe." "Take care, brother," said the biggest Billy Goat Gruff. "Remember the fearsome troll."

"If our little brother wasn't scared of the troll, then neither am I," said the middle-sized Billy Goat Gruff.

So, the brave goat went to the bridge and started to cross it. His hooves were heavier than the smallest goat's and they made a heavier trip-trap, trip-trap sound on the bridge.

The troll's voice came from the darkness under the bridge. It was a gibbering, jabbering, slavering kind of voice. "Who's that trip-trapping over my bridge?" he said.

The troll leapt out from under the bridge. "A bigger billy goat, eh? I'm going to gobble you up for my dinner!"

"Wait," called the middle-sized Billy Goat Gruff. "I may be bigger than my brother, but if I eat the grass on the other side of the bridge, I'll grow fatter still."

The troll was hungrier than ever. But he hadn't got any less stupid, either. "All right," said the troll. "You may pass. But I will eat the very next billy goat who crosses my bridge, no matter what size he is."

So the middle-sized Billy Goat Gruff trip-trapped across the bridge and munched on the sweet grass in the field with his little brother.

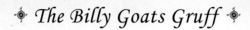

It wasn't long before the biggest Billy Goat Gruff decided to find out what had happened to his two brothers. He went to the bridge and started to cross it. The biggest Billy Goat Gruff was very heavy and his hooves went TRIP-TRAP, TRIP-TRAP on the bridge.

The troll called out from under the bridge and, in his growling, grunting, grumbling voice, said, "Who's that trip-trapping across my bridge? Whoever you are, I'll gobble you up for my dinner." He leapt onto the bridge, but the troll stopped suddenly when he saw who was walking across.

The biggest Billy Goat Gruff was enormous. He had big, shaggy legs with great, big hooves on the end. On his head were gigantic, curved horns. The biggest Billy Goat Gruff wasn't at all afraid. "Go on," he said, in his big voice. "Gobble me up for your dinner, if you dare."

Now it was the troll's turn to be afraid. The biggest Billy Goat Gruff was even bigger than he was. The troll hesitated for a moment, but then he remembered how hungry he was. He leapt at the big goat, but the biggest Billy Goat Gruff didn't care. He ran at the troll and butted him hard.

The troll flew off the bridge and into the fast-running stream. The stream carried the troll far away, down the mountain and he was never seen again.

"That's the end of that," said the biggest Billy Goat Gruff. He trip-trapped over the bridge and joined his two brothers. The three Billy Goats Gruff ate all the grass they wanted and became very fat and they lived happily ever after in their lush, green meadow.

Puss in Boots

Once, there was a miller who had three sons. When it was time for them to go into the world and seek their fortunes, he gave the first son his mill, the second son his donkey, but he had nothing left for his youngest son. "All I have is my cat, Puss," said the boys' father.

So, the youngest son set out into the world, with only the cat for company. "I'll surely starve," he said, sadly.
"No you won't," said the cat. "I will make you a prince, master, if only you'll get me a pair of boots."

The miller's astonished son used the last of his money to buy the cat a pair of shiny, leather boots. Then the cat went into the woods and caught a fine rabbit. Instead of taking it to the miller's son, he travelled all the way to the palace and presented it to the king himself. "It is a present from my lord," said Puss.

The king was impressed. "Who is your lord, little cat?" he asked.
The cat made up a grand-sounding title. "He is the Marquis of Carabas," said Puss.

Month after month, Puss caught the best rabbits he could find and took them to the king, who grew more and more pleased with this mysterious Lord and his cat messenger.

Meanwhile, the miller's son had hardly any food. "When do we eat?" he said. "I've had nothing but crusts for weeks."

"Just go down to the river for a wash," said the cunning cat, "and you'll be surprised."

So, the miller's son went to the river by the big bridge, to wash himself. The cat knew that the king was passing by in the royal carriage with his beautiful daughter. When the carriage rumbled onto the bridge, the cat called out "Help, help, the Marquis of Carabas is drowning!"

The king's servants rushed to the miller's son and helped him out of the water and into some fine new clothes. He was put in the carriage with the king and the princess. The king was delighted to meet the Lord who had been sending him so many gifts and the princess thought him very handsome, too.

"But what will we do now, Puss?" whispered the miller's son. "The king will soon find out I'm penniless!"

"Leave it to me," purred the cat and ran off up ahead. He saw the people of the land mowing in the fields. "Quick!" the cat cried. "The king is coming. If you don't tell him this land belongs to the Marquis of Carabas, he'll chop your heads off!"

The people were so afraid, they did what they were told. When the king asked whose land it was, they all said, "It belongs to the Marquis of Carabas."

Next, the cat came to a mighty castle. Puss knew that an ogre with magical powers lived there. The cat knocked at the door and the fearsome ogre answered. "What do you want?" the ogre boomed. "I am busy preparing a great feast."

"Is it true, mighty ogre," asked the cat, "That you can change yourself into anything?"

"It is," said the ogre. "Watch." Suddenly, the ogre turned himself into a terrible roaring lion, who chased Puss all around the castle.

Finally the ogre became tired and changed back into his own form.

"That's very good," said the cat, "but I bet you can't turn yourself into something small, like a mouse."
"Of course I can!" bellowed the ogre. He turned himself into a tiny mouse and straight away, Puss jumped on him and ate him up!

Just then, the royal carriage rolled up to the door. "So, is this your castle, Marquis?" asked the king to the miller's son. Before the miller's son could reply, Puss said, "Yes, Your Majesty, it is, please step inside."

The king marvelled at the splendour of the castle and so did the miller's son, who'd had no idea of Puss' plan. While they ate the magnificent feast the ogre had prepared, the princess whispered something to her father. The king said to the miller's son, "Marquis of Carabas, I would be honoured if you would take my daughter's hand in marriage."

So, the miller's son proposed to the princess and they were married within a week. The miller's son became a prince and the cat was rewarded with as many mice as he could eat – and a new pair of even brighter, shinier boots.

After that, the miller's son, the princess and Puss lived happily ever after.

Robin Hood and Little John

A long time ago, the outlaw Robin Hood and his band of Merry Men, lived in Sherwood Forest. They robbed the rich to feed the poor people and always fought for justice against the evil Sheriff.

One fine summer's day, in Sherwood Forest, Robin was making his way back to the secret glade, where he and his outlaws had their camp. A broad stream ran across his path. The only way across the stream was to climb over a large log that had fallen across it.

As Robin stepped onto the log, he saw another man do the same from the other side. This man wasn't dressed in green, like Robin. He was wearing furs, like a hunter. He was the biggest man Robin had ever seen – almost a giant. The man carried a great oak staff that was even taller than he was.

"Stand aside!" shouted Robin Hood. "There is only room for one to cross this log."

"No, you stand aside," the large man shouted back. "I am on my way to meet the famous outlaw, Robin Hood. I want to join his Merry Men and I must not delay."

Robin laughed, "I can test this great hulk's strength and courage and see if he's worthy of my outlaw gang," he thought to himself.
"Man-Mountain," he yelled back. "I say again, turn aside and let me pass!" Robin carried a staff like the big man's and he waved it threateningly.

"If you will not turn back, then we must fight," said the man and he charged forward. The two men met in the middle of the log and began to swipe their staffs at each other.

Robin managed to jab the man's belly with his staff, but the man just laughed. "Are you trying to tickle me?" he asked. The big man swung his staff at Robin's feet, but Robin saw the blow coming. He jumped up in the air and the staff swung underneath him. Robin landed on the log, as lightly as a cat.

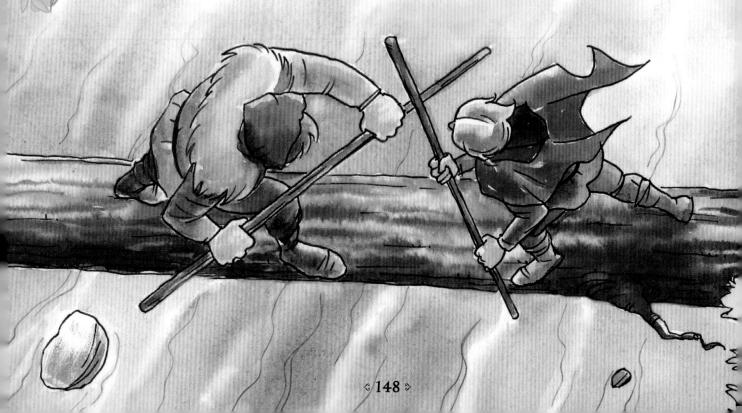

As they struggled, Robin asked the man, "Are you as handy with a bow and arrow as you are with the staff?"

"Yes," said the man. "I can hit an apple from a mile away."

"Hmm," thought Robin. "Perhaps this man is worthy of joining my band." But already the big man was twirling his staff again and Robin had to lean back to avoid a heavy blow.

"You smell like you need a bath," chuckled Robin. "Allow me to give you one," and he knocked the big man sideways with his staff, trying to push him into the stream.

The big man was so strong, the blow from Robin bounced right off him. He didn't even wobble. Instead, he tried to pelt Robin with blows. Robin ducked and jumped so fast that all the blows missed.

The two men battled on and on, but neither could win. Robin was too fast to hit and the big man was too heavy to topple.

Finally, Robin put all his strength into a massive swipe at the big man's belly. The man wobbled and slipped and began to tumble. But, as he fell, he delivered a last blow at Robin's legs, which sent Robin flying into the stream.

Both of the fighters sat in the stream, wet and weary. "Well done, my friend," said Robin Hood. I have never met anyone who could beat me in a fair fight before."

"We both won and we both lost," said the man, laughing. "And now, I must seek Robin Hood."

Robin Hood put his fingers to his lips and let out a long, shrill whistle. It was the secret signal to his Merry Men. Suddenly, the woods around the stream bristled and shook and a group of men emerged.

Will Scarlet clambered onto a high branch, dressed in red. The minstrel, Alan-A-Dale, sprung from the undergrowth, ready to compose a ballad about the fight. Friar Tuck appeared from behind a tree, nibbling on a chicken leg. They had all been watching the contest with excitement. "We are here, Robin," they called.

"You are Robin Hood?" said the big man in amazement, as they climbed out of the stream.
"Yes," grinned Robin, taking his green cap off and bowing.

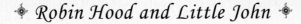

"I suppose I can never join your band," said the big man, sadly, "now I have knocked you into a stream."

"What do you think, my Merry Men?" shouted Robin to his gang. "Should this great fellow be allowed to join us?" All the Merry Men clapped and cheered and shouted, "Yes."

"Welcome," said Robin. "Your strength and courage will be of great help to us, what is your name?"

"I am a woodsman, named John Little and I seek revenge on the sheriff for stealing my land," replied the enormous man.

Robin put his hands on his hips and laughed heartily. "You have a strange name for such a giant. I think we'll call you Little John."

So, from that moment on, John Little became known as Little John. He joined Robin Hood and his band of Merry Men, who robbed the rich to feed the poor and fought for justice against the wicked Sheriff.

Little John had many exciting adventures and lived a long and happy life in Sherwood forest.

The Pig That Flew

Once upon a time, a poor farmer and his wife lived on a tiny farm by a brook. The farmer tended his sheep, while the farmer's wife grew vegetables in their little garden. Life was hard for the farmer and his wife and they rarely had enough food to eat.

One day, when the farmer's wife was selling vegetables at the market, she saw a man selling a piglet. The piglet had small, stumpy wings made of white feathers, like a goose's. "All the other pigs have been sold, but nobody wants one with wings," said the man. The piglet looked very small and sad.

The farmer's wife took pity on the piglet. "I'll buy it," she said. "When it grows up, perhaps we can fatten it up and eat it?"

So, the man tied some string around the pig's neck and gave it to the farmer's wife. "You never know," he said, "this pig may make your fortune, one day."

To the farmer's wife's surprise, the piglet fluttered up into the air. She had to hold tight to the string to stop it flying away. The farmer's wife carried it back home on the end of the string, like a balloon.

The farmer wasn't very pleased when he saw what his wife had spent their last pennies on. The farmer's wife took the piglet off its string inside the farmhouse.

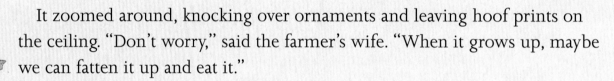

It zoomed around, knocking over ornaments and leaving hoof prints on the ceiling. "Don't worry," said the farmer's wife. "When it grows up, maybe we can fatten it up and eat it."

It wasn't long before the flying pig grew so large, it was too big to keep in the house. The farmer took it outside and let it go. "I'm sorry," said the farmer to the pig, "But we can't afford to feed you any more." The pig took off and flew away over the hills.

The next morning, the farmer and his wife were woken up by grunting noise, outside their window. The flying pig had returned. He had a bronze chain in his mouth. "I suppose he can come back, if he behaves himself," said the farmer.

The farmer sold the chain and had enough money to buy food for a while. The farmer even built the pig a sty.

Soon enough, the money ran out, so the farmer's wife went to dig up vegetables to sell at the market. But all the vegetables were gone. The pig had eaten every last one.

The farmer angrily took the pig to the top of a high hill and chased it off. The pig fluttered its wings and flew away, sadly.

But the next morning, the pig was back and this time it had a silver necklace in its mouth.

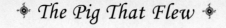

The farmer let the pig stay in the sty again. "But if he does anything else, he's gone for good," said the farmer. He sold the necklace and again they had enough food for a while.

Only a few days later, the farmer went to get the sheep from the fields. He found the pig flying through the air, chasing the sheep in all directions. It took the farmer hours to round them up. When he got back to the farm, the farmer was so angry, he chased the pig around and around the sty. The pig flew away over the hills in fright.

The next morning, the pig was back again, with a gold crown in its mouth. "Where does it go?" the farmer's wife wondered.
"I don't care," said the farmer. "Tomorrow, we'll take it to the market and sell it. Someone else can fatten it up and eat it. Then we'll be rid of it for good."

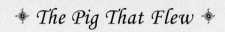

That afternoon, a gigantic storm raged over the farm. The farmer rushed inside. "I must get the sheep to higher ground," he said to his wife. "The river is flooding and they will all be drowned."

The farmer tried to reach the sheep, but soon the water was so deep that he couldn't move out of the house. Water began to pour in through the doors and windows.

"We must climb on the roof, or we'll drown!" said the farmer's wife. When they got up to the roof, they saw an amazing sight. The flying pig had flown over the flood. He was swooping over the sheep, guiding them to the hill where they would be safe.

The waters rose and rose, until they were lapping at the roof. "We're doomed," said the farmer. But the pig flew onto the roof and landed next to them.

The farmer and his wife climbed on the pig's back and the pig flew off, just as the waters covered the top of the roof.

The pig flew a great distance until he landed by a mountain cave. Inside, there was a pile of treasure. "This must be where the pig was getting his presents from," said the farmer. "We're rich!"

The farmer and his wife never had to work again. They lived happily ever after – and so did the pig that flew.